ABOUT THE BANK STREET READY-TO-READ SERIES

More than seventy-five years of educational research, innovative teaching, and quality publishing have earned The Bank Street College of Education its reputation as America's most trusted name in early childhood education.

Because no two children are exactly alike in their development, the Bank Street Ready-to-Read series is written on three levels to accommodate the individual stages of reading readiness of children ages three through eight.

○ *Level 1:* **GETTING READY TO READ (Pre-K–Grade 1)**
Level 1 books are perfect for reading aloud with children who are getting ready to read or just starting to read words or phrases. These books feature large type, repetition, and simple sentences.

○ *Level 2:* **READING TOGETHER (Grades 1–3)**
These books have slightly smaller type and longer sentences. They are ideal for children beginning to read by themselves who may need help.

○ *Level 3:* **I CAN READ IT MYSELF (Grades 2–3)**
These stories are just right for children who can read independently. They offer more complex and challenging stories and sentences.

All three levels of The Bank Street Ready-to-Read books make it easy to select the books most appropriate for your child's development and enable him or her to grow with the series step by step. The levels purposely overlap to reinforce skills and further encourage reading.

We feel that making reading fun is the single most important thing anyone can do to help children become good readers. We hope you will become part of Bank Street's long tradition of learning through sharing.

The Bank Street
College of Education

For Bennett

– G.B.K.

For Jacob Harmon Lieberstein

– S.A.

WHO GOES OUT ON HALLOWEEN?
A Bantam Book / September 1990

Published by Bantam Doubleday Dell Books for Young Readers
a division of Bantam Doubleday Dell Publishing Group, Inc.
1540 Broadway, New York, New York 10036.

Special thanks to Betsy Gould and Erin B. Gathrid.

The trademarks "Bantam Books" and the portrayal of
a rooster are registered in the U.S. Patent and Trademark
Office and in other countries. Marca Registrada.

Library of Congress Cataloging-in-Publication Data

Alexander, Sue, 1933–
Who goes out on Halloween?

(Bank Street ready-to-read)
Summary: Enumerates the various creatures out on
Halloween, from fat monsters and pirates to small witches and ghosts.
[1. Halloween–Fiction.   2. Stories in rhyme].
I. Karas, G. Brian, ill.   II. Title. III. Series.
PZ8.3.A378Wh 1990   [E]   89-18468
ISBN 0-553-05891-6 (hard cover)
ISBN 0-553-34922-8 (trade paper)

Published simultaneously in the United States and Canada

PRINTED IN THE UNITED STATES OF AMERICA

0 9

Bank Street Ready-to-Read™

Who Goes Out on Halloween?

by Sue Alexander
Illustrated by G. Brian Karas

A Byron Preiss Book

BANTAM BOOKS
NEW YORK · TORONTO · LONDON · SYDNEY · AUCKLAND

Who goes out on Halloween?

Tall witches.
Small witches.

Any-size- at-all witches.

Striped clowns.
Spotted clowns.

Even polka-dotted clowns.

And some mini-bunnies.

Ghosts go out on Halloween.
Look! Here is one.

Who goes out on Halloween?

Any-size-at-all pirates.

Striped cats.
Spotted cats.

Even polka-dotted cats.

And some mini-monsters.

Space people go out
on Halloween.
See? Here they come!

Three by three,
and four by four!

Everyone goes out
on Halloween!

Witches and clowns walk
side by side.

Bunnies and ghosts look for places to hide.

Pirates and cats
walk in a row.

Monsters and space people
see who they know.

They go by twos
and threes and fours.
They climb up steps.
They knock on doors.
They hold out bags.